WITH  S0-BMV-898

Powered is published by
Stone Arch Books, A Capstone Imprint
1710 Roe Crest Drive
North Mankato, Minnesota 56003
www.mycapstone.com

Library of Congress Cataloging-in-Publication Data
Names: Sridhar, Priya, author. | Owenson, Meg, illustrator.
Title: Novice / by Priya Sridhar; illustrated by Meg Owenson.Description: North
Mankato, Minnesota: Stone Arch Books, [2019] | Series: Sci-finity. Powered |
Summary: Kelli's powers of telekinesis, and her ability to speak to and understand
inanimate objects has often seemed to mess things up, including causing her father
to desert her and her mother; but now he is trying to get back into her life, and
she is torn between anger, resentment, and maybe hope, emotions that are not
improved when he immediately dumps her off at a tennis day camp, where one of
the older girls seems to want to humiliate her—a situation that leads her to use her
powers (with the enthusiastic assistance of her tennis ball and racket) to retaliate,
and ultimately causes her to blow-up at her neglectful father.
Identifiers: LCCN 2018044105| ISBN 9781496578860 (library binding) |
ISBN 9781496578914 (ebook pdf)
Subjects: LCSH: Psychokinesis—Juvenile fiction. | Extrasensory
perception—Juvenile fiction. | Fathers and daughters—Juvenile fiction. | Children
of divorced parents—Juvenile fiction. | Anger—Juvenile fiction. | Tennis resorts—
Juvenile fiction. | CYAC: Psychokinesis—Fiction. | Extrasensory perception—
Fiction. | Fathers and daughters—Fiction. | Anger—Fiction. | Emotions—Fiction. |
Tennis—Fiction. | East Indian Americans—Fiction. | LCGFT: Paranormal fiction.
Classification: LCC PZ7.1.S718 No 2019 | DDC 813.6 [Fic] —dc23
LC record available at https://lccn.loc.gov/2018044105

Editor: Gina Kammer; Designer: Ashlee Suker;
Production Specialist: Kathy McColley

Printed and bound in the USA.
PA49

NOVICE

BY PRIYA SRIDHAR

ILLUSTRATED BY MEG OWENSON

STONE ARCH BOOKS
a capstone imprint

FIC
RID

SPYGLASS
UNIVERSITY
We watch. We see. We learn.

Kelli Paramar

PROJECT EPIPHANY
ATTN: John Herenhoff, PhD
Department of Psychology
Psychometry Research Facility,
Wing 2A
The University of Spyglass

CASE FILE #006-KP
By T.E. Hoffer
Test Subject: Kelli Paramar

Kelli was recommended for this study based on her unusual
scans during her volunteer psychological surveys. Kelli
Paramar is thirteen years old and is an eighth grader at Adaline
Rosenstein Middle School. She lives with her mother, Marjan
Paramar, who agreed to Kelli's participation in the study.

CURRENT SYMPTOMS:
Kelli claims she has the ability to talk to inanimate objects.
Most of the time, Kelli reports, the objects talk back. If Kelli
talks to an electric current directly, it will cause the device
and the current to go haywire. More tests are needed to
understand the extent of Kelli's abilities.

TEST SUBJECT HISTORY:

Kelli found herself in trouble when she tried proving her abilities to her father, Sanjib Paramar. Kelli used to believe she got her powers from a toy telephone that she reports talked back to her as a child. Refusing to believe her, Sanjib threw away the phone. Later, Kelli accidentally crashed his computer while trying to prove her powers existed. Her father reportedly left the household sometime after. Her mother believes that Kelli's abilities are only part of her imagination. Kelli states that she hasn't told anyone else about her abilities since her parents' divorce.

PERSONAL AND SOCIAL DETAILS:

Kelli reports enjoying video games, especially role-playing games. Her favorite subjects in school are art and history. Her least favorite is math.

Marjan Paramar is a psychologist-in-training, hoping to become a private therapist. Currently she works as an instructor at Spyglass University, and she is working toward a PhD in psychology.

Sanjib Paramar is a chemical engineer who now lives in a different city. Kelli and her father do not visit often. Kelli reports mainly staying in contact via phone or email

Kelli has one close friend, Al (full name, Abd al-Rahman). His family comes from Pakistan. They've known each other since the start of middle school and both love video games. However, Kelli reports that he doesn't know the truth about her powers, and she doesn't know if he would believe her.

CHAPTER ONE

Kelli wasn't sure why her mother looked so nervous. They had been sitting at an outdoor table at the local gelato place with two bowls between them. Kelli's bowl was topped with a waffle chip and sprinkles while her mother's had a few chocolate chips.

"I'm glad we were able to get here right when it opened," her mother said. "It isn't often that we're able to make time for this place."

Kelli had to agree. The gelato place was tiny, with a few round tables meant for two people, and only one person worked behind the counter. Usually people waited in a long line to grab their favorite flavors.

Her mother hated the wait, though she liked the gelato. Kelli knew that something was up if her mother was willing to risk the possible crowds to get some of the city's best ice cream. That fact meant that her mother either had bad news or really great news that was too big for their small condominium.

"Amma, what is it?" Kelli asked, using the term for "mom" that was common among Indian kids.

"It's an email. From your father," Amma said.

Kelli's stomach dropped. She shoveled another spoonful of gelato—strawberry swirl—into her mouth to deal with the sinking feeling. She and Amma never talked about Appa, unless it was about summer plans or camps.

"What now?" Kelli asked. "What does he want?"

"Kelli, don't be rude," Amma chided her. "It's nothing he wants from me. He wants to spend some time with you over the summer."

To prove her point, she pulled a printout from her messenger bag. It showed a receipt for a plane ticket to

Fort Palm, a city name that Kelli didn't recognize. If her mother weren't holding the papers, Kelli would have ripped them up, tossing them away with the used ice-cream bowls and wooden spoons.

"It's not like he deserves politeness," Kelli said, mostly to the papers. "He gave me up. He said he didn't want me. So what is it? Is it about child support?"

"No," the printout responded in a matter-of-fact voice that seemed to vibrate. "It's not about that."

Her mother pinched her lips before answering. She, of course, couldn't hear the paper's reply. Amma didn't have powers to talk to objects like Kelli did. She didn't even believe such powers existed. She popped a large chocolate chip into her mouth. Chewing sounds filled the awkward space between them.

"He didn't say he didn't want you," she said. "He felt he wasn't willing or able to take responsibility for an excitable child."

"Same difference," Kelli said in her most brittle tone.

"Kelli, please—" Amma began.

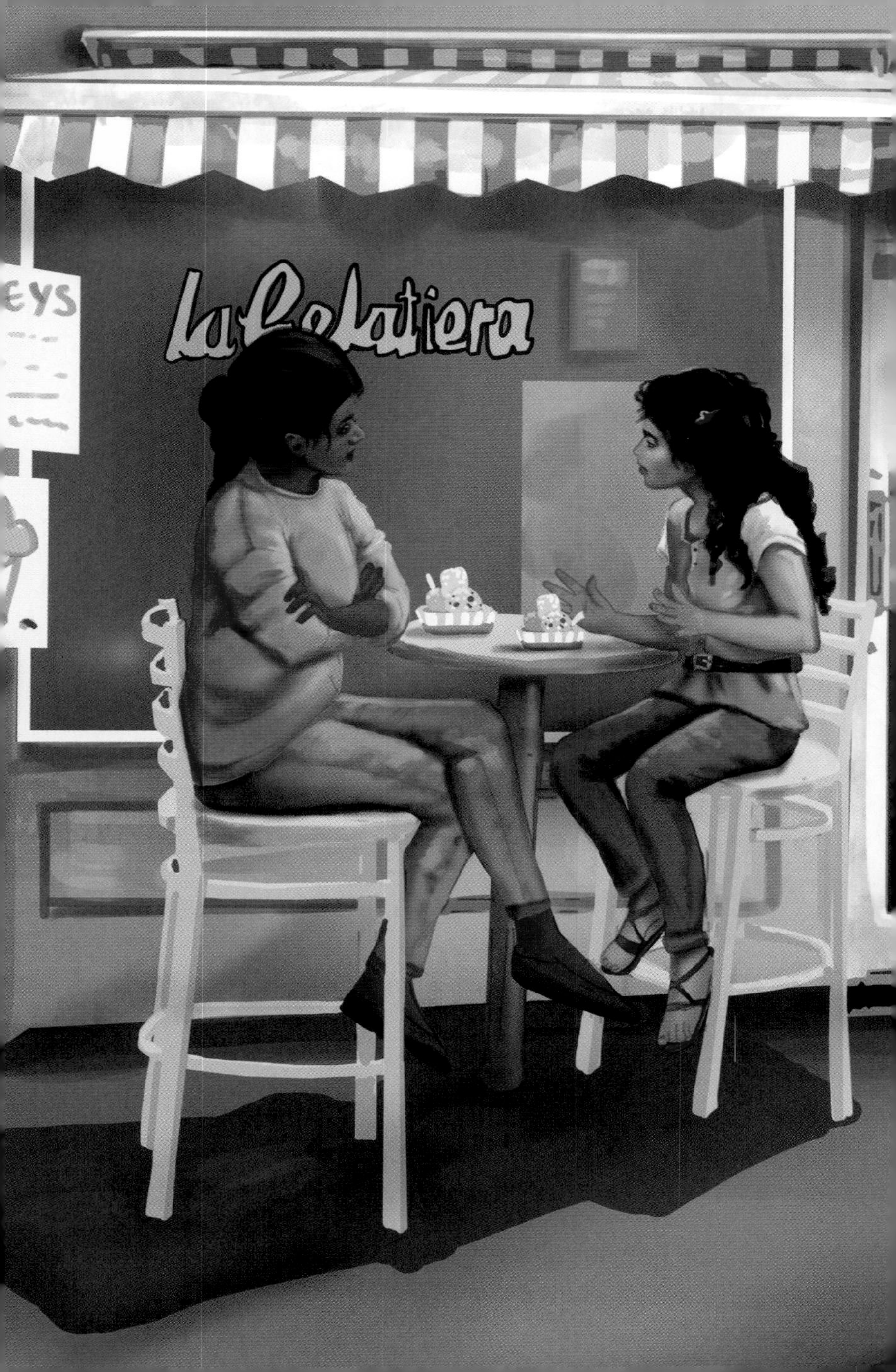
EYS
La Gelatiera

"It *is* about child support, isn't it?" Kelli glared at her waffle chip. "Well you can tell him that he may as well—"

"Kelli," her mother now looked angry. "Trust me, that didn't even come up in the email he sent. Your father may have his flaws, but he's not greedy in that sense."

It was rare for Amma to say anything bad about Appa, or about anyone.

"Flaws?" Kelli said. "He left us! He left *you*! That isn't a flaw. That's a bad decision!"

"I'm with the kid on that," the printout chimed in.

Worse than a bad decision, Kelli's father had caused a lot of chaos in her young life. She hadn't realized trying to tell him about her powers and how her toys could speak with her would end their relationship. But then he had tossed half her toys in a garbage bag in a rage over her "nonsense" and put them in the apartment dumpster. Then he left, leaving his set of keys on the counter.

She'd been six years old. Later, Kelli had stopped checking to see if he had come back for his keys. Then it had finally sunk in that her father wasn't returning for them. He had never picked up any of his things. Kelli kept her powers secret after that.

"He seems to have changed his mind," Amma said. "I honestly don't know why, but he is your father. And he wants to see how well you have grown."

"Pass," Kelli said flatly. "If he wants photos and growth charts, we can email them to him. I'd rather spend time with you and with Al for the rest of this summer."

Her mother gave a weak smile. She chewed another cherry and spat the pit into a napkin. "I will take that as a compliment. But don't you want to know him? At least to see if you can have that relationship as you grow."

"Look, I know what this is about," Kelli said. "You're going to say that one day I'm going to regret not knowing my father on his deathbed and all that. But that only works if the person is worth the effort.

Appa isn't worth my effort—or time. He left. He just doesn't get a free pass because he's feeling the guilt he should have felt when I was younger."

Amma frowned. Kelli angrily picked up a waffle chip and bit into it. The crunch seemed deafening in the mostly empty parlor.

"You can tell him I'm not coming," she said. "He's never even apologized for leaving."

"He already bought the plane ticket for you," Amma said without argument.

"That's why you brought me here?" Kelli narrowed her eyes. "This was a bribe. Of course. Why didn't I see it coming?"

Her mother was good, she had to admit. If they had been at home, Kelli would have flown into a tantrum for even considering the idea. In the shop, the gelato helped soften the blow.

"I wasn't trying to trick you," Amma said.

"No. You were trying to deliver bad news in a good way." Kelli chewed on a waffle chip slowly.

"Kelli, I'm not saying you have to stay with him forever," Amma said. "It's just one week—one week for him to prove that he's changed. I'm just worried that you'll regret denying him this chance. The divorce was bad, and I'm worried that all the anger I felt has also poisoned any chance of a relationship you may have with him."

"Trust me, Amma, you didn't," Kelli shook her head. "The poisoning was all on his side."

"Kelli—" Amma pleaded.

"Has he apologized?" Kelli leveled eyes with her mother. "Did he actually say he was sorry for leaving us in the lurch and making us leave our old apartment?"

"In the email, yes," Amma said, handing the printout to her.

Kelli scanned the printout. She studied the words above the barcode for the plane ticket. They were written in complete sentences, addressing her without any nicknames—too polite and stiff to make up for a lifetime of not being there except on the phone. And even then, Kelli didn't like talking to her dad. It was always so awkward, so stilted.

"Don't I have a choice?" she asked, staring at the pages, already sensing that she didn't. Amma didn't answer right away. She looked thoughtful, like she was figuring out what words to use.

"You don't," the printout responded. "You most definitely do not have a choice."

"Hmm." Kelli squinted at the email. She couldn't believe the apology was sincere, even if the signature did read *Sanjib*.

"Promise me you'll try first to work things out with him. And in return, if he ends up being terrible, call me, and I'll change your return ticket," Amma promised.

That didn't make Kelli feel better.

CHAPTER TWO

The night before she would fly to Fort Palm, Kelli lay awake in bed. She tended to have trouble sleeping, but that night was even worse. Her legs cramped and woke her up, making her groan and rub them in pain. She kept rubbing them, even as it became clear that it wasn't helping.

"Are you OK?" her pillow asked.

"No," Kelli said bluntly. She looked at the ceiling and studied all the cracks.

"I'm coming with you," her pillow responded in its soft, muffled voice. "It's a new place, and you'll need comfort."

Kelli couldn't help but smile. At least something was on her side. And she *was* taking the pillow. If her father tried to throw it away, she would cause many doors to slam in his face. She had become good at whispering to doors and getting them to do what she asked.

"You know I'm going to pack you," she said. "Amma's giving me a travel pillow for the flight, but you're staying in my bag."

"You don't need another pillow," it said with a huff. "I can comfort you well."

"You can argue with my mother about it," Kelli snorted. "I don't have any choice in going. Besides, planes are supposed to be dirty. You can stay clean."

"Who cares about dirtiness?" the pillow asked. "It's not like you've washed my case in the last week, even though your mother asked you to."

"Do you want me to toss your case in the washer?" Kelli asked.

"Nah, it's too late," her pillow said. "If you were going to wash me, you should have tossed me in the wash with your clothes. Besides, that wasn't my point. You don't need another pillow."

Kelli sighed. She sat up and hugged her pillow. The cotton pillowcase had a hole. The pillow was only trying to help. It had always helped.

"It won't be for long," she said. "Just for a four-hour flight. Nothing could replace you."

. . . .

The next morning, Kelli's legs were still cramping, and she had dark circles under her eyes. Part of her wondered if she could use the cramps as an excuse to get out of going. But Amma had insisted that they needed to be on their way. Kelli was going.

The drive to the airport was short, at least. Her mother put jazz on the radio, and they listened in silence. Kelli leaned against the car window and wondered if a traffic jam would cause them to miss her flight. But it was an early morning flight on a Sunday, so traffic wasn't terrible. No dice.

Kelli tried not to think of the man she was meeting—her Appa. At best, she had memories of watching him shave or of him making some hot chocolate for her after a nightmare. Those memories weren't enough to take away her anger and confusion about why things had gone the way they had.

There was a parking space at the airport for drop-offs. Amma parked, took a ticket, and helped Kelli take out her roller suitcase and her Tetris-themed duffel bag.

Her mother took her as far as security, then they agreed that Kelli would be fine making it to her gate from there. They began their goodbyes.

"Now stay safe," her mother said, before hugging her. "Text me when you board and when you land. I've put forty dollars in your wallet, which should be enough for a cab in case he's not there to pick you up. The hotel address where he's staying is in your phone. If you need to come home, call me, and I'll put in the return fee."

"It will be fine," Her pillow whispered from within the duffel bag. That made Kelli smile. It was going to be awful with her father, and it wasn't as if her best friend, Al, could go with her. Kelli had even asked both her mother and Al's parents, but it was supposed to be "family time." Al *was* family to Kelli, but he wasn't the type of family that her mother meant. Which sucked.

Thinking of him, Kelli texted Al. It helped her feel less alone. She let him know she was leaving, and she added a sad face emoji for good measure. Al already knew that she didn't like her father and that she didn't want to go. She shifted her suitcase handle to her left hand and trudged along. It slanted to the side and started rolling on one wheel. She angled her body and tried to walk.

You doing OK? Al responded.

I guess? She texted back. *We weren't running late to the airport, which is always a good thing. But also, I hate this. I hate this a lot.*

I can't believe your mom is making you go, he said, and Kelli could almost see him biting his lip angrily. Al continued, *She could have at least given you the* choice. *He may be your father, but he hurt you. He hurt both of you.*

Don't I know it, Kelli responded, rolling her suitcase along. *If it weren't for the fact that I don't know the city, then I'd try to change the plane ticket to go to Silicon Valley and sneak into game testing sites.*

If she tries to make you visit him again, you bargain for a trip to Quo Headquarters, Al advised. *I heard they're doing an entire virtual reality theme park.*

Kelli snorted. Gate numbers hung on the corridors. She didn't find getting around difficult. She just had to follow the signs. She checked each of them until she found her gate. People crowded the metal chairs, leaving only one free by a garbage can, and there weren't any outlets near it to charge her phone.

She sighed. *Trust me, I would rather be in a virtual world than in this one,* she texted Al.

Kelli waited as her plane was boarding. She had only been on a plane once, but she remembered what to do. She and her mother had gone to visit her grandparents in India over the winter holidays. That hadn't been too much fun. The cities were hot, even in the dead of winter, and the most you could do was meet relatives at social gatherings, travel by train or car to various tourist sites, or ride in boats along the rivers.

For the life of her, Kelli didn't understand why people would want to go to India. She didn't see the romantic culture depicted in films. All she had found was jetlag, some really spicy food, and nosy aunts and uncles asking about her future plans.

Yet when other people talked about their travels, they said they found kind faces and "spiritual energies" that ran in currents through the villages. Kelli didn't even find spiritualism in the temple statues when she used her powers to talk to several of them.

This time Kelli would have a shorter plane ride. Fort Palm was a four-hour flight.

Kelli boarded with the other passengers and settled into her seat. As it took off, Kelli felt a little queasy. She calmed down once they were in the air and studied the other passengers. Most people wore headphones and read books or Kindles and typed away at their laptops. Some kids were playing with their parents' phones. Kelli turned to gaze out the window at the sky.

The plane ride soon made Kelli want to doze. She had her own phone and plenty of games to play on it, but the truth was that she was too exhausted to even play her favorites. Yet she couldn't get herself to fall asleep. The travel pillow that her mother packed was comfortable—it was filled with memory foam and oddly seemed to hold itself together—but the dread of what would happen after the plane landed on the tarmac in the resort city of Fort Palm wouldn't let her relax. And, of course, she hadn't slept the night before. So she just ended up feeling miserable.

"Just my luck," she murmured to her travel pillow. "My first big adventure alone, and I am scared and tired."

"It's going to be OK," her travel pillow said. "I may be new, but I know that's what you want to hear."

"What about it is going to be OK?" Kelli muttered. "I don't want to see the jerk. I don't want to spend *any* time with him."

"I heard what your mom said on the way to the airport. If he's making the effort now, then he'll probably try to make a good impression this time," the travel pillow pointed out. "Besides, you have an exit if he ends up being a complete jerk to you and can't even manage to be civil for a week. Your mother promised to help if it comes to that, and you have emergency cash. She reminded you about all of that."

Kelli made a face. The pillow had a point. Amma wouldn't leave her stranded in the middle of a strange city with someone she hadn't seen for years. . . . Had it really been that long?

The Fort Palm airport was large and had many sea creature sculptures hanging from various points in the ceiling. A blue lobster the size of a Labrador dangled upside-down. An octopus with glasses worked at solving a puzzle cube.

Kelli grabbed her suitcase and tried to balance her duffel bag on top of the rolling bag. It tilted back and forth.

"You didn't have to stuff me on top of your old pillow!" The travel pillow complained. "It's breathing in my ear!"

"I can't breathe. I don't have a nose!" the pillow retorted.

"Then stop pressing onto me, you goose-feathered lug! I can feel all your body weight!" The travel pillow huffed.

Kelli rolled her eyes. Just what she needed: two comfort objects bickering with each other. It was hard enough trying to make sense of all the new airport signs.

"Do you mind?" she asked. "Pipe down. You can argue when I unpack you at my dad's place. Don't distract me right now."

The pillows stopped talking. Kelli glanced at her duffel bag, adjusting its weight and tying one strap to the suitcase handle. She was wondering if she could buy another plane ticket to go to that virtual-reality park Al mentioned.

Of course, her mother wouldn't allow that, and forty dollars wasn't enough for a plane ticket. Maybe a bus ticket, but that was about it. Kelli didn't even know how much a bus ticket would cost or how far it would get her from the airport. Besides, Kelli had promised her mother she would try not to run away.

Then she reached the arrivals pickup area, and her last-minute doubt was interrupted by panic. She saw her father there standing in line, waiting to pick her up. Kelli forced herself not to run the other way.

CHAPTER THREE

The man she remembered was tall and skinny. The man who was waving to her had a small paunch and seemed to have shortened over the years. He also wasn't wearing a suit or holding his briefcase. He wore a T-shirt with a panda on it lying in the sun.

She wondered if time could shrink people. Or maybe it was that Kelli had grown, and it made all of her memories of large things from her childhood seem small.

Kelli wanted to turn around, hop back on the plane, and beg the attendants to take her home. Instead, she walked forward with a stony expression and baggy eyes.

"Kelli-rani, hi!" he said, in a voice that sounded raspy yet excited. "How was your flight?"

She flinched as he hugged her. That hadn't changed at least, the way he hugged. But Kelli wasn't sure if she liked the hug. It felt weird.

"It was OK," she said.

He took her suitcase. She held onto her duffel bag. She didn't want him tossing out any of her pillows. Clothes were one thing since clothes wouldn't likely be tossed away like her toys. But she didn't trust him with her pillows.

"Are you OK?" he asked. "Have you eaten?"

She shook her head. Breakfast had been a lifetime ago, just simple cereal and milk. Amma had packed some snacks, and the airline attendant had passed out bags of salty peanuts, but Kelli hadn't really been hungry. Now she was, but she wasn't sure what her dad was thinking.

"I figured you would be hungry, so I'll order a pizza on the way," he said. "Do you still like plain cheese?"

Kelli did still like cheese pizza. It was pizza, after all. But she felt a twinge of anger at the sense that her dad had put life with her on pause, had pressed the right button on a TV remote, and went on with it when he wanted. He was trying to un-pause and pick up where they had left off. But Kelli hadn't paused. She had kept living, moving, and growing. She didn't need him. And she didn't need him thinking she was still the toddler that talked on her play phone.

"I'll have whatever you're having," she said blandly. "Unless it's not vegetarian."

He sensed Kelli's frostiness, and his smile became more fixed. They walked toward the elevators labeled for the parking garage at a slower pace. Kelli was glad she had told her pillows to stop fighting. Any bickering now about how they had to be duffel bag roommates would drive her over the edge.

"No, it will be a loaded veggie pizza," he said. "I was going to get a small one with olives, red and green peppers, and basil. You are fine with all of that?"

"They're all fine," Kelli said. "I have veggie pizza with Amma all the time. She's good at finding places that have a good veggie option."

He pursed his lips and looked away, ignoring the barb in her tone when she mentioned Amma. Kelli frowned, wondering if she was being too hard on him. He found an elevator button, pressed it, and let her go inside first.

"I remember feeding you olives once as a kid," he said. "That was after you had learned to like Indian curry and rasam. You ate ten of them in one sitting and then said you hated them. For the life of me I couldn't figure out why."

Kelli made a face. She was glad she didn't remember that. But her dad looked so earnest in recollecting it.

"I was a kid," she said, her tone softening. "Kids do a lot of things that don't make sense."

The elevator doors opened. Appa rolled the bag to a red Honda that looked brand new.

"My rental while we're here. Looks good, doesn't it?" Appa asked as he unlocked it.

Kelli got into the front seat. She placed her duffel bag at her feet. The pillows were still keeping quiet, mercifully enough. Her dad punched some buttons on his phone, pulling up an app. Then he placed the phone into a cup on the dashboard that lit up. It looked like a phone charger.

"The pizza should be ready by the time we get to the country club," he said.

"Country club?" Kelli asked. "I thought we were staying at a hotel."

"Oh it's the same thing," he said. "Your mother didn't tell you? I took time off from work so that we could spend the week together at a country club. It has good rooms and plenty of activities for kids your age. The pool also has a giant slide, and plenty of fountains."

Kelli would rather have chewed off all her fingernails than admit to Appa that she liked swimming in large pools. The one at their condominium was always crowded with people wanting to swim laps, and that pool didn't have a slide at all. But the fact that her dad remembered warmed her, and not in a bad way.

"That does sound like fun," she admitted.

Maybe her dad really had changed and wanted to make up for the past seven years. Perhaps Kelli could relax and enjoy this vacation.

⋯⋯⋯⋯⋯⋯⋯⋯⋯⋯⋯

Fort Palm didn't look that different from home. There were palm trees lining the airport exit. The palm trees gave way to skyscrapers and hotels. Then they drove along the coast.

Kelli texted her mother to let her know that she arrived safely. Then she texted Al the same thing. Both of them responded quickly. Her mother's relief was obvious despite the lack of emojis, and Al used many emojis to convey his worry.

Kelli really wished Al was with her. He'd know how to ease her nerves.

Her dad focused on the road, not talking much to her except to ask how school and life were. She told him how exams were but not about the games that she and Al played together. It was none of his business, and what if he didn't care?

Kelli looked out the window. Boats crossed over the ocean waves. They were brilliant white ships of various sizes, some with dozens of portholes, and some no bigger than little sailboats.

Kelli guessed that it was tourist season with so many people out sailing. She began to daydream what it might be like to have her Appa around to do fun things with like sailing. The idea made a sudden hollow feeling pierce her stomach. Kelli blinked quickly as her eyes prickled with the emotion. Kelli surprised herself with how much she wanted those experiences and how much she wanted that love and acceptance from him. She swallowed and angrily shoved her feelings down. Appa had rejected her. Why did she still want anything to do with him?

But maybe, a voice said from deep in her mind, *just maybe I could have the Appa I imagine. Maybe if I can make him like me again . . .* Uncomfortable following the thought further, Kelli returned her attention to the drive.

Soon they reached the beachside country club. Appa pulled into a guard gate. He pulled out a plastic card and showed it to the guard on duty. The gate lifted and let them inside.

"Oh, this looks nice," Kelli said despite herself.

The country club had pinkish walls and curved spires, as well as dozens of lanterns on posts. Her dad parked in a lot marked GUESTS. Then he took out her suitcase from the trunk.

Giant marble steps, as well as a steep ramp, led to the front. Appa led Kelli to the ramp so that he could wheel her suitcase up. Even without going far, he panted. Kelli climbed and pretended that she didn't feel a little out of breath too.

As they walked in, Kelli saw cages with metal birds inside. She could tell they were metal because they didn't move and glinted under the chandelier lights. Part of her wanted to spend time talking with them, to hear their stories. But then she saw her father. She remembered to keep her powers well hidden from him.

"So I'll get a room card for you," her father was saying. "That way if you need to go to the room on your own, you can."

Appa nodded at the woman behind the front desk and walked to the elevators. Shouts of joy came from the bar next to the front desk, as well as a popping sound. Kelli looked quizzically and then shook her head. Grownups. She didn't want to know.

More elevators. These were nicer than the ones at the airport or at her mother's university. Soft music played.

"Tomorrow we'll eat breakfast, and then I can take you to the summer camp," her dad said.

"The what?" Kelli asked.

"Oh, I thought you'd have fun at the sports day camp for kids while I play on the adult tennis courts," he said. "It's a good time of the year for tennis and soccer."

Kelli gave him a funny look. He didn't notice. Anyone who knew Kelli knew that she wasn't a sports person.

"Aren't we supposed to be spending time together?" she asked.

"We will," he promised. "I just don't want you to be bored while I meet with a few investors."

"Investors?" she asked.

"I've got my business to keep up," he said. "Even on vacation. So I have a few people I need to meet with tomorrow."

Kelli didn't even know how to respond as the elevator stopped. The sliding doors opened on a polished corridor with plush carpets. Appa went to the room nearest to the elevators. He opened it up by pressing his key card to a black square.

"We'll get you settled," he said. "Then the pizza should be here soon."

"Yeah. Sure," Kelli said.

He heard the dullness in her tone. His eyebrows rose, but he didn't say anything else before he went into the bathroom and slid the door shut. Kelli found the nearest outlet, pulled out a charger, and plugged in her phone.

She tried to take a few calming breaths before she had to face her father again. *It'll be fine*, she tried to tell herself. *Just one day while he's busy, then it'll be better.* She hoped.

* * *

Kelli didn't talk to her pillows until the lights were out for a while. She didn't want her dad to catch wind of what she was saying. She waited until he was asleep before grabbing her pillows and her key card from the room's desk and walking out into the hallway. She sank to the floor, hugging both her old pillow and her new travel pillow. The carpet was so soft it could just as well have been used to line the beds.

"I don't like this," she said. "Is he really that stupid? Sports camp? Really?"

"He hasn't seen you in ten years," her old pillow said. "I imagine a man like that tends to miss the obvious from phone calls and emails. "

"And what's this about meeting investors? He said he took the time off," Kelli complained. "Does he actually want to spend time with me or not?"

"He wants to. I can sense it," her old pillow said.

"Besides, don't forget, you can tell your mother and you can leave," her travel pillow added. "Then you can use me on the flight back sooner rather than later."

"Don't make it all about you," Kelli's old pillow snapped. "She should be able to make that decision without pressure from a comforter."

"You're one to talk, goose feathers. You want to make this work out even though he's made a terrible first impression," the travel pillow argued.

"I've known her longer! This could be good for both of them," her old pillow insisted. "These things just take time."

"You two fighting isn't going to help," Kelli told them. She told herself again that it was just one day. She could handle the camp that long and then things would get better.

Kelli returned to the room. Appa slept soundly in the other bed, without any effort. Kelli supposed that was the look of a man who was exhausted all the time. Appa used to make Kelli hot chocolate when she couldn't sleep. But that was a long time ago, and now he didn't even realize Kelli could have used some. He seemed to have forgotten what it was like to know when someone needed comforting.

CHAPTER FOUR

The morning was off to a rough start with the alarm clock in the room going off to loud rap music. Kelli hadn't slept well. On top of her usual problems, her father snored in his sleep. It had taken all of Kelli's effort to not to go sleep in the hallway.

Next, her dad rushed through breakfast. They ran into the country club dining room and sat at a table without even waiting to be seated. Her dad then called over a waiter and said they would be getting the buffet.

"All right if I have French Press coffee, Marsala?" he asked, reading the waiter's nametag. It read "Marstall" clearly enough to Kelli. She cringed.

"Sure, but that's not how my name is pronounced," the waiter said with dignity. "It is pronounced 'Marstall.' Would you like cream and sugar?"

"Sure, Marsala," said her dad, still pronouncing his name incorrectly.

Kelli gave the waiter an apologetic look. It seemed her dad was one of those people that didn't know how to treat waitstaff well. Her mother would have insisted on ultimate politeness and kindness.

"Thank you, *Marstall*," Kelli pronounced his name with emphasis. "You're being a big help to us. I would like a glass of orange juice, please, if that would be all right."

Her father gave her a startled look. She was certain he hadn't expected any anger in the morning before coffee. But she hadn't slept, and she knew part of it was his fault.

The buffet mainly had bacon, ham, and sausage. Kelli wrinkled her nose. There was a tray filled with scrambled eggs, but eggs on buffets were always cold and chewy. Kelli turned away. She managed to find a basket full of croissants and Danishes.

"That seems to be a lot of starch," her father commented. "Are you sure you need all of that? It doesn't look healthy."

"Then maybe you should have asked for vegetarian options," Kelli said nastily as she buttered her plain croissant.

Her father didn't say anything else. Marstall returned with the coffee along with cream and sugar. Her dad poured the cream daintily, before stirring in two sugar packets. It made the coffee a light brown. Her mother always drank coffee black.

"So what sort of investors do you see?" Kelli asked, after she had swallowed some food and felt less angry and tired.

"Mainly business investors." Her father drained half of his mug in one gulp. "I am starting a small company developing apps for translating languages, and that requires investors."

"Who, exactly, are these investors?" Kelli asked.

"People willing to buy shares of my company and provide money for me to develop the apps," he said. "Before we can buy any of the software we need, we need to have the money. And right now we only have a fraction of it."

Part of Kelli wondered if there had been a child support argument. Kelli almost felt pity that her father had to brown-nose rich people. Kelli had seen her fair share of rich people that could throw money at anything and make problems go away. Al's uncle was one of those people. He had been nice enough, but he always seemed to miss the obvious, as if money clouded his eyes.

"Hmm. And they also play tennis?" she asked casually.

"Yes, they do." He gave a weak smile. "They think that the French champion has good odds this year in the Australian Open, even with his recent knee surgery. It's amazing how the games play out, especially during tournaments."

His eyes lit up, the first time he actually looked enthusiastic. Kelli tried not to take offense that he found tennis more interesting than he found her. It was only day two, technically. She didn't want to spend all their time fighting. But oh she was so tempted.

Kelli sighed quietly and remembered the calm sailboats. She decided to try to meet her dad halfway. "Tell me about the Open," she said, sipping at her orange juice.

He started pulling up articles on his phone, showing her photos of various athletes. Kelli tried to show interest and to ask questions. If she could show him they had something in common, maybe he would try harder to spend time with her. Maybe he could like her again. It was what her mother would advise for trying to befriend someone. And in this case, if she befriended her father, maybe it would help with that aching feeling of loss in her stomach.

Kelli thought it was a shame that her father had chosen a *sports* camp for her. On the way through the country club to the outdoor courts and fields where the camp was being held, Kelli had spotted what looked like a computer lab with a 3D printer. They also passed a library filled with fancy bookshelves and polished wooden round tables. While her father had to kiss up to people, she could have learned to print 3D sculptures.

The bright red tennis courts were set close to the water. In fact, Kelli could feel a sea breeze. She had to admit that was pretty cool. A few large banners advertising luxury tourist attractions hung on the court fences. The tennis courts also had basketball nets, and one side had foul lines drawn in white paint.

Kelli could also see the soccer fields, and she made a face. A huge mesh net covered one end of the field, tied to several mangroves. It looked like a fancy prison, even though she could tell it was to keep the soccer ball from ending up in the water. Kelli thought the rocks and mangroves beyond the net looked far more fascinating, with all their nooks and crannies. She had learned in class that mangroves could make islands and were nesting grounds for so many creatures. How interesting it could be to explore!

She tore her gaze away as the sounds of the day camp brought her back to her unfortunate reality. A group of kids, all dressed in designer tennis outfits and headbands, warmed up nearby. Kelli instinctively put a hand to her bare forehead and felt embarrassed. She had packed some shorts, but they were only gym clothes from school. A tall woman with a square face and a white visor looked over the kids. She looked up as Kelli and her dad approached.

"Sanjib, hi," she said without her stern expression changing. "I take it this is your daughter?"

"Yes, this is Kelli." he replied. "Kelli, this is Sunee, your counselor."

"Nice to meet you." Kelli shook the woman's hand. Despite the fierce look on Sunee's face, Kelli felt like the counselor was sincere.

"Hi, I'm Virtue," another girl suddenly announced. She bounced up to Kelli's father. "Aren't you going to introduce me, Mr. Paramar?"

Her dad's expression changed. He now looked nervous.

"Yes. Kelli, this is Virtue Haddix. Why don't you say hello?"

"Hello," Kelli said cautiously.

Virtue looked like a pop singer trying to hide undercover and doing a terrible job of it. She had long blond hair with auburn highlights and curled ends, dark blue eyeshadow, and thick lashes that looked professionally done. She also had a button nose.

"Nice to meet you," Virtue said in an overly sweet voice. "It isn't often the day camp gets new members so late into the summer."

Kelli immediately didn't like Virtue. She didn't know if it was her smarmy tone, her arrogance, or her eyelashes. Whatever it was, Kelli preferred being straight up with people. Liars, like some adults she knew, tended to be dangerous. She could already tell that Virtue was going to be an utter stereotype.

"I can tell you two are going to get along," Appa said. "I need to head to the other courts. See you after camp?"

"Yeah, sure," Kelli said, trying to feign enthusiasm.

Her dad strode away. He put on his own headband and visor that Kelli hadn't noticed he had brought with him. She felt even more self-conscious.

"Sunee, why don't I show Kelli the ropes?" Virtue asked the counselor sweetly. "With tennis and all. We have some time before camp officially starts, and I could work on my serve."

"Maybe later, Virtue." Sunee also looked like someone who didn't put up with nonsense. "Why don't you all just get to know each other? Kelli, your dad already ordered a racket, so let's get you set up and see how that goes."

Sunee handed her a beautiful red racket with white strings and showed her how to wrap a black tape called grip around it. The grip felt smooth to Kelli's fingers, and she liked it. Sunee also adjusted Kelli's right hand.

"Have you ever played tennis before, Kelli?" she asked kindly.

"Nah," Kelli said. "Our school doesn't have a program, and I've never taken lessons."

"Then maybe you should step back and learn some basics before scrimmaging," Sunee suggested.

"Scrimmaging?" Kelli asked.

"Playing a match." Sunee gave Virtue a hard look. "After all, a professional does not deliberately take on a beginner when they don't even know the rules."

That seemed fair. Two players faced off against each other. One would serve the ball. Kelli only understood that much of it.

Kelli tried out her racket and swung it. Her hand twisted as she did so. Sunee corrected her grip.

The morning didn't start off too bad. Sunee gathered the kids, told them they would be drilling, and split them into groups to hit the balls over the nets.

Sunee knew who was a beginner and who wasn't. She introduced them and put Kelli in a group with several kids smaller than her, who didn't seem to know the sport any better than she did. They didn't return Kelli's smile and didn't talk to her when she tried to be friendly. They kept sending cautious glances at Virtue.

"Hey, Lauren," Kelli smiled at a girl maybe only a year or two younger than herself. Lauren was also learning tennis for the first time, but she was trying hard. Kelli thought they could try learning together. "Want to partner up?"

The girl looked over her shoulder and saw Virtue watching her. She shook her head quickly. "No thanks. Virtue said she was going to help teach me."

Kelli tried not to grind her teeth. Did Virtue control every kid in the camp? She tried smiling again. "That's fine. She can still teach you. We will just practice for a little bit first. Until she's ready."

Lauren shook her head again. "No. I'd better wait for Virtue."

Kelli shrugged and walked a little farther off to practice on her own. When Sunee was free again, she helped Kelli learn how to hit a ball.

Kelli began to catch on. Even so, she missed more balls than she hit. Oddly enough, Sunee told her "nice try" every time she whacked a ball into a net and criticized her every time she got it over the net. Kelli guessed it had something to do with the quality of her hits.

They took one mid-morning break. Everyone had plastic or metal water bottles, and they took large gulps from them. Kelli went to the fountain and took a long drink. When she returned, Virtue was on the court and waving to her.

"Come on, I want to see how good you are," Virtue cooed.

"Where's Sunee?" Kelli asked.

"My mom's called her to ask about private lessons." Virtue explained. "So how about a quick match while we wait?"

"Funny, I guess you didn't hear what Sunee said," Kelli retorted. "I don't know anything about tennis."

"Oh, I play with every new kid," Virtue stated. "It helps me see how much they're worth."

Kelli shot her an acidic look. The other kids looked scared. It seemed they had also gone through the same routine.

"Yes, and when you beat someone who has no 'worth,' that doesn't add much to yours," Kelli said.

Now Virtue was the one that looked acidic. Kelli glared at her before grabbing her racket and heading to the baseline. Maybe if she just went along with Virtue's strange initiation, the other kids would finally be allowed to play with Kelli.

The sun burned into her back as she took her place on the court. "I've met people way scarier than you," Kelli muttered under her breath. "I know I'm going to suck at this, but I'm not going to be scared."

Kelli tried to bend her knees and squat like Sunee had showed her. She felt so stiff, from head to toe.

Her hair fell over her forehead, and gathered sweat between each curl. The court felt slippery under her feet.

Virtue, in contrast, looked like she had been practicing tennis ever since she could crawl. She took her stance with ease, smiled, and tossed her tennis ball into the air. Then she whacked it, hard. The ball spun through the air and straight into Kelli's thigh.

Kelli yelped and dropped her racket. It clattered to the ground.

"What was that for?!" she shouted.

"Oh, oops," Virtue brought her racket up. "I'm sorry. I was assuming you would know how to run around the ball."

"Virtue," Sunee warned, running over from where she had hung up the phone. "Showing off is very unsportsmanlike."

Kelli rubbed the sore spot on her thigh. She regretted her words about not being scared as she straightened, panting. It wasn't Virtue that scared her;

it was her swing. That ball had to be going a hundred miles per hour. And Virtue had hit her on purpose. Kelli swiped the sweat off her forehead with her hand.

"Now play fairly while I work with the younger kids," Sunee warned Virtue as she left them.

By the middle of the match, Kelli ached all over and was covered in sweat. Virtue had nailed her several times with the tennis ball. After the second time, it was clear that Virtue could hit the ball exactly where she aimed. And hard.

Before tossing another ball back to Virtue, Kelli whispered to it, pleading. "Please, please don't hit me again!" She didn't know how much more she could take.

The ball grunted softly, in what Kelli hoped was agreement. Kelli licked her dry lips. Then she took a deep breath of the hot summer air and got into her stance again.

On Virtue's next serve, the ball slowed as it neared Kelli. It began to spin and curve slightly. Kelli grinned.

The ball was making itself miss her. But that also meant Kelli had time to react to it. Taking the opportunity, Kelli swung her racket, and it connected with the ball. That was the only serve Kelli returned, and it flew way out of bounds. But Kelli still felt the satisfaction of being able to hit one. Sore, tired, and bruised, Kelli finally lost the match without a point to her name. But at least it was over, and maybe the other kids would be allowed to be friendly now.

"Not bad for an amateur," Virtue snorted.

Kelli glared at her and staggered away. She was so hot and thirsty she couldn't bother with a comeback. The water fountain released a cool stream of water. Kelli slurped up as much as she could, but it never felt like enough.

"You don't have a water bottle?" Sunee asked, coming back from her drills with the other kids.

"My dad didn't say I needed one," Kelli said.

Sunee's eyes studied her with pity. She reached into her pocket and took out a dollar.

"Get a bottle of water from the machine," she said. "Your father can pay me back later."

"I can't take that," Kelli said. "I appreciate it, but—"

"You have to. You need to stay hydrated at all times. Especially in this heat." Sunee had a stern look. "We'll play some more tennis before breaking for lunch, and then we'll do some soccer. Sound good?"

Kelli shrugged. She didn't like how any of it sounded. The whole camp was miserable. None of the trip with her dad was going how it was supposed to. She took the dollar.

"Thanks," she said.

CHAPTER FIVE

The soccer field looked like a green pathway to a prison courtyard, with the nets covering the mangroves. Kelli stared at it as she kept strolling along with the other kids. Despite all Kelli's trouble in giving in to Virtue, they still shied away from her. Maybe she hadn't passed Virtue's personal test. Well, that was fine.

"I'm not here to make friends," she muttered to herself. "It's just one day." *And then maybe Appa will spend time with me instead*, her inner voice added.

Virtue still looked very smug as she walked. "Try not to slip," Virtue said. "Those sneakers are better for streets."

Kelli glared at Virtue. She trudged over to where Sunee waited for them. Everyone stopped and gathered around.

"So we're just going to play a simple game," Sunee said. "Pick your teams."

Kelli walked off to the side. She didn't want to be picked at all. And what a lucky day—she was picked last for the team with smaller players. That was fine. It was all fine. Kelli set her jaw.

Sunee threw a soccer ball into the field. Virtue made a beeline for it. Kelli tried to run, but she stumbled. The grass was slippery.

"Aw nuts," she said, not bothering to make it sound sincere as the other kids ran past her.

She had hoped soccer would go better since she actually had played soccer at school, but she had no luck there either. The other kids had the right shoes and shin guards. Her dad hadn't prepared anything for her, except for the racket. The kids on the other team managed to steal balls from Kelli, and she missed every

one of her own team's passes. The more she tried, the angrier she got.

Kelli ran in for a hard kick toward the goal to let out her frustration. A short boy from the other team blocked her out of nowhere. Before Kelli even knew what was happening, the ball slammed up into her face and knocked her completely off her feet. Kelli lay in the grass for a moment, stunned.

"Oh come on!" she yelled at her slippery shoes while holding a hand to her stinging cheek. "I don't even want to be here!"

"We'll ground you!" her sneakers responded. "Come on, get back up," her sneakers said in unison.

"Give me a minute," Kelli snarled at them. Everyone else was on the other side of the field. They had left her to lie on the soil for Sunee to notice.

When camp was over and her father came to meet her, Kelli was all but prepared to call her mother and demand a return ticket. She hadn't wanted to spend time with her father, and she wasn't going to spend all of this visit in a horrible camp.

They went to the country club restaurant. Kelli ordered the largest soda, which her mother never allowed her to do. But her dad didn't argue. So that was one plus. She guzzled it down.

"Do you like camp?" he asked.

"No," she answered bluntly. "I don't play sports at home, except when we have to in P.E."

He didn't seem to understand the sting in Kelli's tone. He looked occupied, as if a recent stress was troubling him.

"It's just a learning curve," he said. "Sports are a good form of exercise."

"Not when there's a camp queen bee doing all she can to make you hate them," Kelli mumbled.

"A what now?" he asked.

"Nothing," Kelli said irritably. "I don't see how it's supposed to be fun when I can't even make progress."

"It's only your first day." He drank a long sip of his fizzy water. "Just give it a chance. I know I was terrible my first time playing tennis. A few more days and you should be fine."

"A few more days?" Kelli asked.

"Yes, you'll be playing for the week—at least through Friday," he informed her. "The camp goes until the end of the week, but I should be free all day Saturday."

"I have to do this for a week?" Kelli said with horror. Any relief from the soda quickly faded away.

"Yes. Some other business matters came up, so that's how long I signed you up for," her dad said, giving her a funny look.

Kelli took a deep breath. One day was one thing. She didn't know if she could handle a week. Her mother would have lots to say about this.

Then Kelli's ridiculous daydream of sailing with her loving Appa flickered back into her mind. The image threatened to bring tears with it. Kelli let her anger back in instead. "Wasn't the whole point of me coming to see you so that we could spend time together?" she asked, unable to keep the frustration out of her tone. "How are we going to spend time together if I'm going to be learning how to hit a stupid ball on a stupid court?"

"It's just during the days," her dad said. "I thought you'd be bored during the time I'd be meeting with investors. We'll still have the evenings. And Saturday before you fly home next Sunday."

Unbelievable. The whole thing was like a nightmare. Kelli's acidic glance apparently didn't dent her dad's enthusiasm. Surely a person couldn't be so oblivious.

"I don't even have any of the equipment that I need for this camp. It's not like the gift shop has soccer cleats, and even if they did, I'd have to try dozens of them to find one that has a good fit. If I had known, I would have talked with Amma about it—like you should have!"

Her dad blinked rapidly, obviously not sure how to react. So instead he just ignored her pain and suffering.

Had it been as hard for him to deal with her attempts to tell him about her powers?

"I guess I should have thought of that," he admitted. "But you don't need cleats to play soccer well."

Kelli stared into the bottom of her soda glass and took a loud sip. It was a noise meant to bother her dad, and it seemed to work.

"But you have a racket, a towel, and a bottle of water it seems," he said. "What more do you need?"

"A plane ticket home!" Kelli shot back at him. "Where someone actually cares!"

He finally seemed to get it. His eyes went wide, and he opened and closed his mouth a few times before he finally said, "OK, OK! I see that you're upset. And I'm sorry I haven't been able to spend more time with you. But let's spend some time together now. We'll finish eating, and then we can go to the hard courts, and I can show you a few things to help you at camp."

That wasn't quite what Kelli had hoped for, but maybe it was a start. At least Appa seemed to be trying to make things right. She finished her drink as he paid for the meal.

The walk to the courts wasn't as bad in the evening. The air was much cooler. Kelli managed to keep pace with her dad, while rubbing at the spots where Virtue had hit her. She was sure that she was going to be black and blue the next day. Then maybe she could make her dad understand how bad camp was.

"We'll use this court." Appa went to one with dim lights. "I'll sign in, and they'll turn on the lights. No one wants to use it because of the mosquitoes."

Ah. Mosquitoes. Of course, there had to be a catch. There was always a catch. Kelli groaned.

"Head over to the service line," he instructed. "Then maybe we can hit some balls."

Kelli scraped the bottom of her sneaker against the green concrete a few times and waited in silence. Her dad grabbed a handful of tennis balls from a basket by a bench, tucked them into his shorts pockets, and came to the court.

"Just a gentle swing," he promised, hitting a low ball over the court. It was gentle enough that Kelli could actually hit it.

A few more balls followed, ones that didn't hit her on the legs. Kelli managed to return each of them.

"Great!" Her dad said. "I think you're doing just fine. You'll be great by the end of camp! I can't wait to see you then."

Kelli made a face. But inside, she dared to feel a twinge of hope. If only she could impress him, maybe he would want to be with her more. *If I can show him I can learn to be good at his favorite sport* . . . Kelli let the thoughts drift away before they became too distracting.

In any case, she had to give her dad credit. Unlike Virtue, who didn't seem to know the meaning of "beginner," Appa sent her easy shots, at the very least. At night, the green hard courts felt more welcoming than the clay ones. With the sun going down and the court lights, just Kelli and her dad, she didn't feel as exhausted and worn out.

She didn't know if she felt happy, exactly, playing tennis with her dad. But it was a type of connection. And he seemed happier on the court than in their room. In fact, he hadn't seemed very happy around her anywhere else.

One week, she promised herself. *Just one week to try to understand him. If that means learning tennis for him, maybe that's not so bad. Then I go home and play a ton of video games with Al. How hard can it be?*

CHAPTER SIX

Early the next morning, Kelli decided she wasn't going to let Virtue bully her off the court or the soccer field. She also decided she would do whatever she could to make sure things weren't as miserable the second time. Talking to the tennis ball in her match with Virtue had given her an idea to get through a week of sports camp. She was never going to magically love sports, but perhaps she could gain some aid in playing them with the use of her powers.

Still, a tiny wave of fear passed over Kelli as she took the money Amma had given her into the country club gift shop. Spending the money meant she was losing her emergency taxi ride to the airport if she needed to fly home early. But Kelli let the wave pass as she reminded herself again that she had decided to stay and try to make things work with her dad.

Kelli slapped all the bills on the gift shop counter to buy a new pair of shorts and a large water bottle. They were completely overpriced, but it was necessary to make sure the rest of her time at camp would go a little better. And if she was going to impress Appa, then she needed all the help she could get. The cashier gave Kelli back just a few little coins. Kelli sighed and put them in her otherwise-empty wallet, taking her bag of new items.

Back in her room, she waited until her dad was getting ready in the bathroom to talk to her racket to get advice. She set it on the bed in front of her. "Racket, what will help me get ready to do better at tennis today?" she asked as she put on her new shorts.

"A heavy breakfast is a bad idea," it told her in a slick metallic voice. "But you'll still need energy. Go with something light like toast and juice. But don't forget your protein. You need to be fit."

Huh, Kelli thought, idly wondering how a tennis racket knew so much about nutrition. But it sounded like good advice. When she and Appa went down to the dining room, Kelli had orange juice, one egg, and toast at breakfast. Her dad seemed to approve.

When they were finished, Kelli raced to the court way ahead of Appa. She wanted time before camp started to try out a few ideas with her powers.

"Hey, wait up!" he called. "See, I told you that you'd like this sport!" He followed her and waited on the side of the court to watch.

She snorted as she went. Some kids were already gathered there.

"Nice to see you here," Virtue told her sweetly. "I'm looking for someone to practice my serves on."

"You can hit at me when camp starts. I have to practice," Kelli retorted with a scowl. She pushed past Virtue and past her stunned look. There was a basket of balls on the clay court. She grabbed it with two hands and carried it as best as she could to an empty net.

"Good," her racket said. "Show no fear."

"Kelli," her father called from the edge of the courts, "that wasn't very nice!"

She glared at him. If only he cared about her feelings as much as he obviously cared about Virtue's! Then she grabbed the first ball on top and tried to remember what Sunee taught her.

"Remember, keep your body straight and perpendicular to the court," the racket advised. "Adjust your grip. Shut out the world."

"OK," Kelli responded. Then she studied the tennis ball in her hand. "How do I do that when the world is here?" She nervously glanced to where her dad stood.

"It takes practice," the ball answered in a rubbery, high-pitched voice. "But that's why you're here. You need to learn to just focus on me. Now practice tossing me, without serving over the net."

Kelli did. She caught the ball. It gave a rubbery sigh.

"No, no, no," the ball complained. "You're not paying attention. See, the issue is you need to toss me straight up. You angle me too much, and that messes up your swing."

"Can't you just go straight up regardless of how I toss you?" Kelli asked, annoyed.

"Well, sure!" it said. "You just needed to ask. Let me show you. Toss me again."

Kelli tossed the ball upward again. This time it chirped as it came straight down. "Good! Now try hitting a serve with the racket."

Kelli did. Her racket hit the ball at just the right time for a perfect serve. The ball smacked into the service box. Kelli grinned smugly and turned.

"Appa, did you see—" she trailed off as she searched for him. But her dad had vanished. He had left right before she had shown off. Kelli ground her teeth. Fine. There would be other times.

Instead of her dad, Kelli caught a glimpse of a blond ponytail disappearing behind one of the closest ad

banners hanging on the fence around the court. Kelli frowned.

"What was she up to now?" Kelli grumbled to herself as well as her racket and another ball from the basket.

The racket made a strange thrumming sound. "She was watching you practice."

"The whole time?" Kelli asked, wondering how much Virtue might have seen—or worse, *heard*.

This new ball clucked in an overly cheerful way. "Well, why not? You're improving so well. The way you tossed the other ball was just perfect!"

Kelli bit back a response as she noticed more of the kids watching her with interest. She pinched her lips shut. Perhaps she had been a little too careless about using her powers in the open. She'd have to try to be more careful. Then again, Virtue already seemed to think Kelli was strange. She was probably just having a good laugh at seeing Kelli talking to herself while she tried to practice alone.

Sunee came onto the courts and called everyone over. Kelli shrugged off the prickly feeling she got from knowing she had been watched. Then she trudged over to join the others.

"OK," Sunee said. "Today we'll run through everything we practiced yesterday, and then we'll work more on group drills and rotate partners." As Sunee gave them their instructions, Virtue kept staring long and hard at Kelli. Kelli tried to ignore her.

Kelli worked through the practices clumsily. While she had made some improvement, she was certain her body was simply unsuited for sports. Playing against the younger kids wasn't so bad, though. But they were still better than she was. So Kelli tried her best, occasionally whispering to a ball to be tossed straight for her so she could actually hit it. That kept the other kids from getting too frustrated with her.

Still, no one talked to Kelli. All the kids whispered to one another and glanced at Kelli to check that she couldn't hear. Then they would smile at Virtue, and she would give them a smile and a nod. While it bothered Kelli, she tried to keep her focus on why she was sticking it out at camp. It wasn't for their shallow friendships or even for the sport itself. She let her gaze linger on one of the sailing ads hanging on the court fence as she waited for her next partner rotation during the drills.

When Virtue's blond hair bobbed in front of her view, Kelli groaned.

"Ready for my serves this time?" Virtue taunted.

Kelli gave her a small grin. This time, Kelli was ready for Virtue. She wouldn't let the stuck up mean girl get the best of her.

"Help me," Kelli muttered to the tennis ball. Then she gave it a perfect toss—with its help—and sent an impressive serve at Virtue's leg.

The ball wasn't anywhere near as hard and fast as those Virtue had hit Kelli with. But Virtue still gave a little surprised shriek as the ball hit. It surprised Kelli too. Kelli hadn't told the tennis and ball to hit Virtue.

She had just asked it for help. But she had to admit that the result was satisfying anyway.

Kelli hid a grin.

Visibly upset, Virtue messed up her toss. It turned her next serve into a dud.

Kelli briefly wondered if getting help from the tennis ball and advice from her racket counted as cheating. But Kelli soon dismissed the thought. She wasn't trying to win anything. She was just trying to survive the camp. And Virtue. Getting a little help couldn't be that bad.

. . . .

The next two days of camp sailed by much easier after Kelli started using her powers to get her through it. Kelli would go to camp, ask all the equipment to help her get through the day, and then, at least on one of the evenings, her dad played tennis with her. She didn't dare use her powers in front of him, so she didn't play very well. But it was when he looked the most relaxed, and they could actually have conversations. Kelli actually managed to sit through an hour of ESPN with him in one of the country club's recreational rooms. She tried to pay attention as he explained why English tennis player Wilhelm Willingham was a favorite, despite being thirty, which was old in the sports world. Kelli nodded and smiled, even asking a few questions.

Unfortunately, Appa kept ruining the few moments he did spend with Kelli by constantly checking his phone or looking over his shoulder. He was always watching for his various investors that were also staying at the country club. Kelli could tell he was worried about appearing cool. She wished she could have told him that dads weren't supposed to be cool, even when they were asking people for money.

Strangely, whenever he wasn't watching for his investors, he kept asking Kelli about Virtue. He wanted to know how she was doing at the camp and how they were getting along. Kelli would just shrug and give him vague answers before changing the subject. The last thing Kelli wanted to do when she actually had a little time with her dad was to spend it talking about Virtue.

Kelli wished he would ask how she was doing instead. She tried to give him the hint. She invited him to watch her in the mid-week scrimmage at camp, but he had failed to show up. If he had, he would have been far enough away that she could have used her powers to play better. But he gave her excuses about meetings coming up and promises to be there next time. Kelli had hoped that if she could show him how she was better at tennis now, he'd want to come to see her more. But the week was almost over, and Kelli would fly home first thing Sunday morning. And Appa had been too busy to see her miraculous improvement.

Kelli grimaced through her frustration as her dad barely took time to say goodbye after walking her to her last day at camp. He was rushing off to meet with a big investor, and he had high hopes.

Worse, Kelli was immediately paired up with Virtue for a drill. Kelli didn't even hesitate to ask her racket and the ball for help. She often wouldn't use her powers when she played the younger kids, but there was no other way to get through playing against Virtue.

The racket and ball did their jobs well. Kelli returned most of Virtue's serves and didn't get hit with the ball once. That kept tripping Virtue up. She missed shots and even the other kids began to notice.

One of the younger girls pointed in shock as Virtue let an easy serve go. If it had been a game instead of a drill, Kelli realized Virtue would have lost. Virtue's face went red as she realized the same thing.

"This is all your fault!" Virtue sputtered at Kelli.

"What is?" Kelli asked innocently.

"I never play this bad, and you're the only new person here." Virtue stabbed a finger in her direction. "You're cheating in some way. I know it. You do something to the ball. I heard you talking to it. You told it to help you, and it did!"

Kelli paused. It was the first time anyone ever pointed out the weird things she could do so directly.

"To cheat at tennis, I'd have to care about it," Kelli said, trying to sound calm. It was mostly true. She wasn't really trying to win. She just wanted to survive.

"Oh, and what was that serving? You were definitely trying. Except you're not actually that good," Virtue snorted. "Not really. So you had to be cheating."

"I'm not trying to win anything," Kelli said. "Why would I cheat? Maybe you're the one who cares too much about winning."

"You can do things. Strange things. I know you're different somehow!" Virtue shouted. She marched right up to Kelli.

"Don't try me." Kelli stood up, clenching her water bottle tightly. "I've been through a lot this summer and I can assure you that you can't scare me."

They glared at each other. Kelli prepared for Virtue to grab her hair and start pulling in the exaggerated way characters sometimes fought in movies.

"Girls!" Sunee marched over. "Do not even think about it."

"She's cheating!" Virtue pointed at Kelli. "No one like her gets good at tennis in a week."

"Maybe no one is as bad as you," Kelli snapped back.

"*Girls*," Sunee interrupted.

But Virtue shouted over her. "It's true! Kelli can do strange things! It's not normal! Whatever she tells the ball to do, it does. I've seen it! Honest! She's making it so none of my shots go where I aim. That *never* happens."

"Enough!" Sunee stopped Virtue, exasperated. "None of that's even possible. I don't see how Kelli could have cheated. I think you're just letting your dislike for each other get the best of you, and that's what's messing up your game."

"But—" Virtue protested.

"No," Sunee insisted. "We'll settle this matter for good. You two can work this out in a one-on-one match tomorrow, *under my watch*. We'll just do a best-of-three games. Then we'll see what's really going on, and if it turns out to be nothing, you put this to rest. Both of you." Sunee looked sternly at each of the girls in turn.

"Hey!" Kelli objected. "It's not my fault she's messing up. Why should I have to play her again? You already know she's a better player."

"My decision is final," Sunee said in a dangerous tone. "You'll both play, and then this will be over. Got it?"

"Fine," Kelli said grudgingly. Virtue finally nodded too, keeping her mouth shut.

"Excellent." Sunee gave them a warning look. "Keep apart from each other for the rest of the day. We don't need all this anger on the courts."

Kelli steamed on the inside and sipped at her water. Virtue huffed and turned away. Sunee shook her head and went to check on the younger kids.

"Shoes, tie your laces together," she whispered at Virtue's sneakers. Then Virtue stormed away, tripping instantly. It was worth it to hear the startled scream.

CHAPTER 7

When Kelli's dad picked her up at the end of the day, he looked irritated. Virtue for some reason seemed smug. She busied herself packing up, but she kept watching Kelli's dad. Most of the other kids had left, and Sunee was organizing the rackets on the bench.

"Kelli," her dad said in lieu of a greeting.

"Hey," she said. "You're right. I'm actually getting the hang of this." *Which you should have noticed by now.*

With his one look at her, Kelli dropped the amused tone.

"Virtue's been complaining to her parents that you're causing problems at the day camp," he said.

"She says you've been cheating at sports and messing her up on purpose. Is this true?"

Kelli whipped her head back toward Virtue. The other girl wasn't watching, but Kelli saw her smiling.

"No," she said. "I'm just trying to learn whatever I'm supposed to learn here."

She was irritated. It was hot, and despite playing better, with or without her powers, her dad hadn't noticed. Just like he hadn't noticed she wasn't a sports person.

"Virtue's parents said she wanted more friends at camp. I thought you'd get along!" he said. "Why couldn't you be friends? Your mother said you were very sociable. Why would you cheat against her?"

That was it. Any pride Kelli felt at improving fell away. Rage replaced it.

"Are you serious?" she said. "And just how would I cheat?" she asked. "Did I pack any body-building steroids? Am I greasing her tennis racket?"

"Kelli, this is serious." He looked angry.

"I'm not cheating," she lied. Maybe she was cheating a little bit, but that wasn't the point in her anger. "I don't even care enough about the sport to cheat. What, you think that just because the queen bee isn't queen of the court anymore that I'm to blame? Maybe it's because she's never had to work hard for anything in her life that she can't stand one loss."

Those were harsh words, but Kelli felt too angry to regret them. Virtue looked appropriately shocked. She stood up from her pretend packing and came over in a huff.

"I'm not a queen bee!" she protested.

"No, because queen bees are actually useful." Kelli was acidic. "Unlike you."

"Kelli!" Appa looked angry now.

"It's the truth," Kelli said, her anger growing.

"Call me a name again, and I'll tell my parents to not fund your company," Virtue broke in. She turned on her heel, her blond ponytail whipping over her shoulder as she stalked away.

That stopped Kelli's train of thought. She was genuinely bewildered. But then the pieces clicked together, and everything made sense.

"You were just brown-nosing Virtue's parents for money?" Kelli asked, staring at Virtue's blond ponytail bobbing away. "That's why you wanted me to come and do these dumb sports? To be friends with her? So you could butter them up? You never even wanted to spend time with me, did you? Tell me. Why did you really want me to come here?"

"I wouldn't say brown-nosing." Her dad looked stern. "And I didn't—"

"And of course you don't even see that she's a bully," Kelli continued. "You only want her parents' money to fund your stupid company. You just wanted to use me."

"That's not true!" he protested "Please let me—"

"I've been spending this whole week trying to get your attention by learning this awful sport, trying to *talk* to you, and you can't even manage that." Kelli blinked so that she wouldn't cry. "You even forgot that I hate sports. Amma could have told you that I'm terrible with soccer at school. I've only been doing this stupid camp because I thought it would make you happy. But you're just as miserable as you were the day you left!"

"Kelli—" he tried to say.

"And that's after you left for seven years. All because I was claiming my toy telephone was talking for real." Kelli made a fist. "Parents don't leave just because their kids are too hard to handle! And I had gotten used to you being gone, because I had to get used to it! It's not even like you had fallen out of love with mom or cheated on her. You left because of *me!*"

Her voice became a screech. Kelli took harsh, ragged breaths. She could hardly hold back the tears— the screams of anger.

"Kelli, that's enough," Appa said, looking terrified and guilty. "Don't make a scene."

"OK, you know what?" Kelli took a deep breath. "Be quiet, *Dad*. You don't have a right to judge what I'm doing or not doing."

Her father looked startled. Perhaps it was the rage that Kelli felt bubbling inside of her. Maybe it was the way he looked over his shoulders, for investors that would drop him for his daughter making a scene.

Kelli decided she didn't need to hear any more from him. "No. I've let you do enough." Kelli turned away. "Amma should have made you refund the ticket. I should have known better than to believe you had changed. You just wanted use me to get money. Someone who leaves a kid because of their imagination doesn't deserve second chances. I'm leaving. I'm asking Mom for a return ticket home for tomorrow. I don't care if it's one day early. We are done."

To emphasize her point, she turned on her heel and walked off the court. Her dad called after her. She ignored him.

He had enough time to follow. The fact that he didn't told Kelli all she needed to know.

The country club had a scenic walk along the water. Kelli stomped, angrily texting Al. He wasn't responding, which must've meant he was with family. She also texted her mother.

If it was a movie, her father would be following her. But it wasn't a movie. He had let her go. Just like she had expected.

Her phone rang. She answered. It was her mother.

"Hi, Kelli." her mother sounded stressed. "Where are you? Are you safe?"

"I'm fine." Her tone was short. "I'm still on the country club grounds. I didn't run away. Yet."

"Kelli!" Amma sounded ready to crawl through the phone to stop her.

Kelli sighed. "Don't worry. You can track me on my phone, remember. But just so you know, I won't be hopping a bus. I'd rather fly home anyway."

"But it's almost time for your flight home anyway. Can't you wait one more day? After a whole week, you shouldn't run away from this," Amma said.

"You can't change my mind," Kelli said irritably.

Amma sighed. "I knew it wouldn't be easy, but you promised you'd try to work things out."

"I tried. Things didn't work out. Dad's a liar. You have to let me come home," Kelli said shortly.

"That bad?" Amma asked.

"Worse than that," Kelli replied.

"He just messaged me," Amma said. "He's worried about you. What should I tell him?"

"Tell him I'm out for a long walk. Why did you make me come in the first place? He's just using me so he can look good in front of his investors," she said.

Amma groaned after a startled pause. "I didn't want my judgment of him to ruin what you thought of him. I haven't had a high opinion of your father in a long time, but I try to keep that from you."

"He's a jerk. Your opinion was right," Kelli stated.

"Not all the time. I married him, after all," her mother said. "And I stayed with him. Whatever happened, he's still your father."

Kelli grumbled. Amma had a point. But it wasn't like traditional Indian society would have tolerated her mother leaving him first. Her grandparents had even asked why her mother hadn't stopped her father from walking out on them.

"But that's what parents are supposed to do," Kelli said. "Stay together. It wasn't your fault he decided to be an irresponsible jerk."

Amma didn't have a response for that. "You need to go back to him. He's worried."

"He didn't look so worried when I walked out," Kelli remarked bitterly.

"Kelli," her mother said with frustration. "At this point, I don't think I can get you an earlier flight. I'll see what I can do, but otherwise just do your best to stick it out one more day. Use it to try to make things better so you don't leave on bad terms. For now, he's still responsible for you. You'd better go back to him."

"I will," Kelli said flatly, "when he stops being a huge jerk. But I need some time away from him."

"I'm going to tell him where you went." Amma was firm.

"Fine," Kelli sighed before hanging up.

She thought about catching a taxi to the airport on her own. She would just wait there for the next flight Amma could find for her. But then Kelli remembered she'd already spent all her money hoping to impress her dad. Or, really, to make him want her more, and that had been for nothing. She had wasted it on him, and now she had no way out. Kelli picked up a stone and angrily flung it down the walkway.

The walkway had various clay sculptures placed along it. There was a flock of flamingos made of green clay. They looked so lifelike. She paused to look at them.

"How long have you been here?" she asked them.

They chirped at her like actual flamingoes she had seen in videos. Kelli felt her mood lift.

"For only a few months," the one lifting its beak to the sky said. "They change the decorations to change with the seasons. We're here now because the local zoo has a new flamingo chick."

"Huh." Kelli did not know about the zoo. She would have loved to see the chick. Sadly, Kelli wondered what other wonderful things the city held that her father had hidden from her. Hidden from her so she would think the sports camp was the only option. So he could use her to get his investors.

"I want to bathe in hot springs volcanoes!" the smallest one chirped, breaking into Kelli's downward-spiraling thoughts. "Do you think we can?"

"Maybe," she said. "You'd have to free yourselves first." But Kelli doubted that was possible. Just as it didn't seem possible for her to find a way out of her mess. Not even her powers could help her do that.

Footsteps and panting. Kelli turned and saw her father jogging toward her.

"Oh, so you decided I was worth coming after anyway?" she asked irritably. "That might have been nice when you decided to leave the first time."

"I'm sorry," he said. "This wasn't my intention."

She gave him her fiercest glare.

"I still talk to inanimate objects," she said, glancing at the flamingoes. "I just don't pretend they're alive."

Because she wasn't pretending. She knew she was giving them life. It still made him uncomfortable, though, she could tell. He shuffled nervously.

"That wasn't why I left," he said. "Is that what you thought?"

"My mother said you couldn't handle raising an 'excitable' child," she retorted. "And apparently you still can't."

"I shouldn't have put you in the camp," he admitted. "And I meant to spend more time with you . . . get to know you better. I knew work would come up, though, and I thought you wouldn't want to sit through meetings while I was talking to investors all the time. And I wouldn't blame you for that."

"And it didn't have anything to do with me befriending Virtue?" Kelli spat.

"I thought it would work out," he said lamely. Then he tried again. "I had thought about having you visit me this summer anyway, but the Haddixes mentioned they'd be vacationing at this country club with their daughter and other potential investors. They invited me to join them and bring you along to meet their daughter. I couldn't resist such an opportunity. And I really thought it might be fun for you, especially since Virtue is your age."

Kelli grimaced. She'd been right. He was using her, though he didn't seem to see what was wrong with that. That was very like her dad.

"The only reason I agreed to come here was because Amma thought you deserved a second chance. And then I was stupid enough to think that maybe you did, and that if I just tried harder to make you want me again, it would be worth it. But do you deserve a second chance?" Kelli shook her head, not knowing what she could believe about him anymore.

They stared at each other for a few moments. Kelli could hear the flamingos trilling away.

"I know I didn't make the best choices in all this, but I'd like to think I do," he admitted. "Maybe you could give me a third chance so I can prove it to you?"

Kelli was too skeptical to answer.

"How about this. What did *you* want to do while you were here?" he asked. She thought about it.

"It'd be nice to see some of the sights in the city," she said. "There's a beautiful place for sailing . . . and there's that museum and planetarium. I'd like to go there if it's not too crowded. And the zoo." She glanced at the flamingoes.

"Done," he said. "We can check on the weather, and there should be time for at least a couple of those."

That seemed like a start, but it almost seemed too easy. There had to be a catch.

"But first, Sunee said you would be playing a match tomorrow to show Virtue you're not cheating," he said. "Why don't I come to that and see how you play?"

And there it was. The thing she had wanted before but didn't want now. She didn't want anything to do with Virtue or the sports camp. She scowled. "No. I won't do it."

Appa sighed. "I'm sorry. I wish I could say you didn't have to. But it's the only way to prove you weren't doing anything wrong. Even if you don't care anymore, can you just play once more for me. Please? Then you never have to again."

"Fine," Kelli growled. "But you don't have to come," she said with more scorn than intended. "Virtue is going to win, like she always does. Then you can still make your deal with her parents, and I can't be blamed." She glared at him.

"I'll come," he said, more firmly and wincing against the barb. "Since you've been working so hard. Now how about we head back? It's getting hot."

Kelli nodded, feeling numb.

CHAPTER EIGHT

Kelli's pillows kept bickering as she stretched in the hotel corridor. Her dad was sleeping inside. She had gone out to get away from the mouth breathing.

"You honestly think you can provide advice when she doesn't even take you out?" her regular pillow said.

"I am out now," the travel pillow retorted. "And some comfort you've been. You weren't able to prevent the fight!"

Kelli sat with her legs splayed from side to side. She moved to each side, so that her fingers could brush the tips of her toes. However, stretching probably wouldn't help her much on the court.

"No one can prevent a fight like that," her regular pillow said.

"You two," Kelli said with exasperation. "Have you considered that all your arguing isn't helping me with my problems? You're both supposed to be comforting!"

That shut them up. Kelli resumed her stretching. She still wasn't that flexible. But maybe it would be enough to keep her from aching all over. Of course, it couldn't stop the aches on the inside.

Footsteps. Kelli looked up. Virtue was pacing in elegant pink silk pajamas.

"I don't want to hear it," Kelli growled.

"Hey, you're the not only one with sucky parents," Virtue said before stalking away.

Kelli glared at Virtue's back. She couldn't understand how rich parents could be sucky.

* * *

Kelli made sure she had her water bottle, and she went onto the court early to practice her serves.

Her dad had still been sleeping since it was only seven on a Saturday morning.

"What am I doing wrong?" she asked her racket.

The racket thrummed. "Tighter grip, keep your stance solid but flexible."

Kelli tried. She did all she could to make sure she was ready. Her dad finally wanted to see her play? Well, she would show him.

A vengeful part of Kelli wanted to do everything she could to make it look like she was cheating just so her dad wouldn't be able to make any deals with Virtue's rich parents. But some strange part of Kelli, hidden deep down, still thought she might have a chance to make Appa really want her if she could impress him with her skills at his favorite sport.

It was ridiculous, she knew, but she couldn't help wanting to fill the aching hole inside her. The blame and anger that panged her so often for driving her dad away in the first place refused to stop, though Kelli always knew it was really his fault. On top of all that,

Kelli had her own selfish desire to win—to beat Virtue in front of everyone and show her what it was like to be bruised and humiliated.

Overflowing with mixed feelings, Kelli tossed her first practice ball. She whacked it over the net, and then she tried another one. It was another really hot day. Kelli could feel a new layer of sweat already begin to coat her body. Still, it was just one more day. One day, and then she wouldn't have to deal with this stupid sort of game anymore. She hadn't even picked up any breakfast, because she didn't want to spend the morning staring at her dad and trying to figure out if he actually wanted to spend time with her.

Virtue stepped onto the court as Kelli managed to get her fourth serve over the net. She watched with narrowed eyes. Kelli ignored her.

"All those serves are way out of bounds," she called. "Are you going to hog that court all to yourself?"

"Help yourself." Kelli pointed to the basket of balls. "I really don't care either way."

Kelli left to get water. Virtue started serving. All of her serves were right on the service line, barely avoiding going out. Kelli considered asking all the tennis balls to assist her with perfect serves again.

All too soon, Sunee arrived. Kelli heard her heavy tennis sneakers and took it as a signal to grab one of the long pink tubes and start picking up balls. This was the only part of the game she really enjoyed, putting order to the court. It also gave her an opportunity to whisper inside the tube.

"How do I at least not lose badly?" she whispered to the tennis balls.

"We'll make sure you can return all the serves," they responded. "You might even win."

"No need," Kelli said. "But what advice can you give me?"

"Trust us," the balls responded in a rubbery unison. "Trusting your own body is a bad idea."

That wasn't reassuring. But she didn't have any other options. She just wanted to survive the

humiliation of the match, prove she wasn't cheating—
though she technically had been cheating—and go
home. Home to her mother, who wouldn't dump her
at a stupid camp before checking the details. Home to
Al, who wouldn't let any bullies isolate her. Home to her
apartment, which wasn't full of strangers.

Some kids gathered to watch, but Kelli's dad hadn't
come. *Fine*, she thought. *I don't need him. I never did.
I'll just do this on my own.* Kelli unloaded the balls into
the tennis basket. She pocketed a handful.

Kelli got the first serve. She tried to line up her body
with the court. It was all about posture and strength.

"Trust me," the ball said. "Relax."

Except she couldn't relax. She had too much
pent-up frustration. That frustration in turn gave her
an odd desire to try to win—to prove she could do it her
own way.

She tossed the ball perfectly in the air, with its help.
She managed to whack it over the net, where it barely
made it into one of the service boxes. Virtue got it easily

and hit it at a sharp angle. Kelli sprinted to the ball, but she didn't reach it in time.

"Go left!" the ball called as it was whacked into the court.

Now you tell me, Kelli thought.

"You got this," her racket said. "She just got lucky."

"Love, fifteen," Sunee called.

Kelli stretched. She may not have cared about tennis, but she still wanted to make Virtue sweat. She decided to let her powers help her all they could. She thought it would be worth the satisfaction of possibly even winning in the end, just to get back at Virtue for all her bullying. And Kelli had one last match to do it.

Kelli served again. This one was a stronger serve, but it went out of the service box. She took a deep breath, dug into her pockets, and pulled out another ball. She tossed it in the air, and aimed. It had a nice angle that Virtue ran to get.

"Go right!" The ball hollered at her, the wind distorting its voice. "Now left!"

Kelli listened. This was useful. They managed to get a rally until Virtue accidentally hit it out of bounds. That was fine.

"Fifteen, all," Sunee said. "Come on, get on with it girls. You get three games, and then we have to move on."

Kelli smirked. It was worth hearing that to see the increased ferocity on Virtue's face. The other girl was getting angry. Anger was a good thing. It meant that Virtue would make more mistakes.

Her third serve was better. Virtue had to sprint for it. Still, Kelli also had to work to make sure she didn't lose the point. They were hitting for a while.

They hit a deuce, at 40 all. Kelli paused for a moment to catch her breath. She looked up, and saw her dad on the sidelines. So he had come to watch her play after all. But rather than watching Kelli, he was talking eagerly with Virtue's parents. Kelli shook her head. She should have known this match was still all about business for him. He wanted his daughter's name cleared for his own benefit.

Kelli gave him a pointed look. Then she returned to focus on her serve. This one was wobblier, and Virtue easily got it. If Virtue got one more point, she would win. But with the help of the ball and her racket to give Kelli some perfect plays, she could change her odds.

Kelli debated. If she used her powers a little more, she could win and have the satisfaction of beating Virtue. She could win, and maybe that would finally get

her dad's attention. She could finally impress him, and he'd have to want her.

Kelli tightened her grip on her racket, raising it near her mouth. She opened her lips to speak to it, but she stopped.

And what would impressing him with tennis do? Kelli wondered. *I hate sports. This isn't even me. Do I want him to want me for tennis?*

Kelli closed her mouth and frowned. She began to question why she cared so much. If her dad only liked her because she won a short tennis match, what did that mean for their relationship? She wasn't a tennis person. If her dad thought she was less of a person because of that, then it was his problem. Why was she doing so much just to try to please him anyway, when he hadn't even made an effort to please her the whole week?

Finally, Kelli made her decision. Then she did speak to the racket. "Stop helping me. Don't do anything for me." She would finish the match on her own, without her powers, even if that meant losing to Virtue. But it didn't mean she wouldn't still try. The difference was in her decision not to play for anyone else but herself.

"All right, girls, switch it up," Sunee ordered. "Time for Virtue to serve."

They switched sides. Virtue served to kill. Kelli, through her own determination, was able to return every serve, but she only managed to score one point in that one. Then they were done.

"All right, that's game," Sunee announced. "Virtue is the winner, and I didn't see any way for anyone to be cheating." She gave Virtue—and then Virtue's parents—a level look.

"Ladies, shake hands. Great improvement, Kelli. You played hard. Especially at the end. I knew you weren't cheating. Wait till we see how you do next summer." Sunee gave Kelli a respectful nod.

Kelli felt a little guilt, knowing she didn't deserve most of Sunee's compliment. But she had worked hard, and she had still played a lot better without her powers than she ever would have imagined. So she decided not to let it weigh her down. She chose to learn from the experience instead.

Kelli went around and started picking up balls from the court. Once they were in the basket, she went to shake Virtue's hand.

"I'll say this," Virtue said, offering her hand grudgingly. "You were working pretty hard at learning a sport you knew nothing about. Not bad for someone who was dumped here. Maybe you'll find reason to come back."

Kelli fixed her with a hard look. Every part of her hurt from the grueling match. But it had been worth playing honestly, at least at the end.

"You're not bad for someone that enjoys destroying anyone that feels like a threat," she retorted. "Maybe that's why you don't have any actual friends."

Virtue looked stunned. Kelli relished it, but she softened her tone to add, "Maybe consider being nicer to people, so you might not be alone." She gripped Virtue's hand and shook it. She kept glaring though.

Her dad had tried to keep his promise, but Kelli still thought he failed. He strolled onto the court, looking very pleased. Kelli didn't think it had been her match that had made him so happy, though. She glanced past him to see Virtue's parents at business on their phones.

"Well! Look at that. You played hard and did well. I knew you could do it for me. I'm proud of you." He placed a hand awkwardly on Kelli's shoulder.

The words sounded hollow in Kelli's ears. After all the time she had spent longing for his approval, it failed to mean anything.

"I didn't do it for you," Kelli shrugged off his hand. "I did it for myself. I did it to show I wasn't scared of Virtue, or you, or anyone else. Just like you shouldn't be so scared of her parents that you can't simply trust in your work to make your business successful. And maybe then you wouldn't have had to rely on using me to get your investments."

Appa lowered his eyes. "You're right," he agreed. "About everything. You're so smart. I should have seen that and listened to you. But all this time I was too caught up in impressing possible investors."

Kelli sniffed, turning away from him.

He moved to meet her eyes. "That's what happened, but it's not what I meant to happen. Though, it was my fault that it did. I promise, I did want to reconnect with you. But I guess I didn't know how. I thought we would play some tennis and everything would be fine. But I don't know anything about the things you really like to do."

"You might have cared enough to find out!" Kelli snapped, though the bite had mostly gone out of her tone.

"Yes," he agreed. "I should have. You tried to learn tennis for me, but I never really tried to do something similar for you. I think . . . ," he paused to choose his next words, "I think we're not very alike, you and I. But I think I'd like to get to know who you really are. I'm just not very good at any of this. I'll need you to help me. Do you think you can try?"

Kelli thought about it. How many chances did she have to give him? But for the first time, she thought his apology was sincere. "I guess I could try," she agreed.

Appa smiled at her—a genuine smile. He seemed to truly see her for the first time. He had finally seen her the way she wanted to be seen. As herself.

CHAPTER NINE

On Sunday morning, it was such a relief to see the airport entrance. Kelli tried to hide her eagerness to get out of the car and check into her flight immediately. Part of her felt sad about leaving her dad, but after such a miserable week, home would be the true vacation.

"Now you stay safe, OK?" Appa said. "Don't get into trouble at home or worry your mother. I think I worried her enough."

Kelli made a face as she made sure she had packed her cellphone. Trouble would always find her. But he didn't need to know that. Not yet, anyway. It would take time, but they could finally start learning more about how to understand each other.

"I'll try," she said. "Try not to disappear for seven years."

"I won't." He looked solemn. "Not this time."

Kelli hugged her father. She tried not to think of how their future visits would go, or how she was sure they would still both make their fair share of mistakes. They may not understand each other very well yet, but at least they knew each other a little better, and that was a start.

"You'll come visit again?" her dad asked.

"Of course," she promised. "Love you."

That last part was a lie. She didn't love him yet. But maybe there would be room for that in the future. Maybe in like ten years.

"Love you too," he said, in a tone similar to hers. It was still better than nothing.

They had shared *something* in their last day together after the tennis match. They took a sailboat

ride, and while it was nowhere near the ideal Kelli had daydreamed, it had been nice.

She had told him about her gaming hobbies and things she did like to do. And after her week at the camp, Kelli understood enough of what her dad told her about his tennis hobbies to have pleasant conversations with him. Afterward, they had spent a little time at the zoo. They had both been fascinated by the baby flamingo, which gave them another experience they could share.

If the whole week could have been more like that last day, Kelli thought she and her dad might have built a real relationship. But in the end, Kelli wondered if that would have been enough on its own. For two people so different, perhaps the only way they could have made any progress was to learn the truths about one another through their mistakes. And after getting through all that together, anything was possible.

Kelli walked through the automatic doors to the airport, with her roller suitcase and duffel bag. Her father waited for her to get inside before driving away.

The way she felt seeing him now held less anger and guilt. Her emotions didn't pang her the way they used to whenever she thought of Appa. That realization made her feel lighter—freer—as she waved to him. As he waved back, she thought she saw a large green flamingo flying in the sky. But maybe it was just wishful thinking.

JOURNAL ENTRY BY
SUNEE VOGUE

My job running the camp at the country club can be very rewarding, but it has its challenges. That's why writing about them is useful. From what I record, I can try to improve and learn from what happens. I want to be a better coach for all the kids that come through the camp. Today was one of those challenging days, but I think it turned out well enough in the end.

When Virtue accused Kelli Paramar of cheating, I was skeptical. Being a coach gives you perspective on people. But I'm also open-minded and decided to watch the court. It wasn't easy. Both girls were giving their best.

As much as I hate to admit it, my gut says that something was happening to the tennis balls. Kelli was interacting them in a way I couldn't see. Perhaps she was commanding them, as Virtue claimed. I can't say for certain, but I could sense something. Kelli kept all her focus on them and not on Virtue.

But I can also say that Virtue was never very great at showing good sportsmanship. She challenged Kelli from the very beginning, and I'm actually surprised Kelli stood up to her as well as she did.

You can only do so much to teach a spoiled kid that they don't own the world. However, Kelli was perhaps the force that Virtue needed to actually realize that she was not living up to her name and being a sweet person. What Virtue will do with that perspective, no one can say.

So even if I were to believe Virtue, I imagine a kid with power over objects wouldn't realize that she would be cheating by using it. She would probably just use it to help her a little when she was starting at such a great disadvantage. Kelli said she didn't cheat. It's not my place to accuse her of lying now, though, and I can't prove it anyway. Kelli lost the match. If she had really cheated, I could only guess she would have won. In any case, I couldn't blame the girl in the end.

Still, Kelli's skills surprised me. You wouldn't expect a kid dumped onto the courts by her father, holding a racket for the first time, to stand up after someone whacked her in the leg, and to whack back. Even having to deal with Virtue, Kelli learned a lot in a week. I wonder what else she could do if she set her mind to it …

I think that if Kelli could find a coach or mentor of some kind who can see what she's really doing, that person could do a better job helping her than I could.

I don't know if there really is such a thing as people with superpowers out there, but if there are, I hope they find trustworthy people to teach them right from wrong in using their powers. That's the only way to help them use such powers for good that I can see.

I hope Sanjib Paramar learns to appreciate that kid. She may have her faults, but I can see she's trying to do what's right. Virtue's parents would have traded anything to have their daughter behave like an actual professional rather than a spoiled brat. Sanjib should realize how good he has it with Kelli. That girl is going to do great things, as long as she keeps her stubbornness. She'll know to fight for what's right, when the time comes.

GLOSSARY

ARROGANCE — an exaggeration of one's own self-worth or importance

DEUCE — a tie in tennis after each side has scored 40 requiring two points in a row by one side to win

DISTORT — to twist out of a natural, normal, or original shape or condition

ESP — extrasensory perception; an awareness of events or facts that cannot be explained by the five senses

GENUINE — sincere and honest

INITIATION — something people are asked to do before being allowed to join certain groups or clubs

INVESTOR — someone who provides money for a project in return for a share of the profits

LOVE — a score of zero in tennis

PSYCHOLOGICAL — relating to the mind

PSYCHOMETRY — the ability to understand or hear things by touching inanimate objects

SMARMY — falsely honest

STEREOTYPE — an overly simple opinion of a person, group, or thing

TELEKINESIS — the power to move objects using only the mind

DISCUSSION QUESTIONS

1. Kelli wants to do well in the sports camp to impress her dad and improve their relationship, but she really hates sports. Was this the best way for her and her dad to get to know one another? Why or why not? Could she have tried something else?

2. Kelli uses her powers to help her get through the sports camp, but technically, she's cheating. Do you think she was right or wrong to use her powers this way? Why?

3. Virtue's behavior is very unsportsmanlike. What do you think might have made her act this way?

WRITING PROMPTS

1. Pretend you are Virtue and write a letter of apology to either Sunee or Kelli for your unsportsmanlike behavior.

2. Pick an object in the room. Write a paragraph describing what its personality would be like if it could talk and what kinds of things it would say.

3. Rewrite the tennis match scene in chapter eight from Virtue's point of view. Think about how her talent for tennis was up against supernatural powers. What would she have been thinking and feeling while playing against Kelli?

Priya Sridhar has been writing fantasy and science fiction for fifteen years and counting. One of her stories made the Top Ten Amazon Kindle Download list. Priya lives in Miami, Florida, with her family.

Priya Sridhar

Meg Owenson

Meg Owenson is a concept artist and illustrator painting and designing for the film and games industry. Originally from Scarborough, England, Meg has been classically trained in illustration and fine art at Leeds School of Art. Notable clients include Sony, Wargaming, Fantasy Flight Games, and Deep Silver.